STINKER'S
RETURN

STINKER'S RETURN

PAMELA F. SERVICE

CHARLES SCRIBNER'S SONS • NEW YORK
Maxwell Macmillan Canada • Toronto
Maxwell Macmillan International
New York • Oxford • Singapore • Sydney

Charles Scribner's Sons Books for Young Readers
Macmillan Publishing Company
866 Third Avenue, New York, NY 10022

Maxwell Macmillan Canada, Inc.
1200 Eglinton Avenue East, Suite 200
Don Mills, Ontario M3C 3N1

Macmillan Publishing Company is part of
the Maxwell Communication Group of Companies.

First edition   10 9 8 7 6 5 4 3 2 1
Printed in the United States of America

Library of Congress Cataloging-in-Publication Data
Service, Pamela F.
    Stinker's return / Pamela F. Service — 1st ed.   p.   cm.
Summary: Alien agent Tsynq Yr, still inhabiting the body of a skunk,
returns to Earth and enlists Jonathan and Karen's help in finding a
souvenir from Washington, D.C., for a threatening space despot. Sequel
to "Stinker from Space."
                    ISBN 0-684-19542-9
    [1. Extraterrestrial beings—Fiction.   2. Skunks—Fiction.
 3. Washington (D.C.)—Fiction.   4. Science fiction.]   I. Title.
    PZ7.S4885Su 1993   [Fic]—dc20   92-21800

for The McKelvey Room Bunch

CONTENTS

Prologue

The creaking of the porch swing mixed with the chirping of insects. Sitting side by side, Jonathan and Karen watched evening creep into the yard. A firefly flickered in the lilacs, another in the shade of the apple tree. A third wavered upward into the deepening blue sky to join the first faint stars.

It's beautiful, Karen thought.

It's peaceful.

It's incredibly boring!

Suddenly the yard exploded with barking: happy, frantic barking. Sancho, Karen's cocker spaniel, burst from the lilac bush chasing an animal. A black-and-white animal. A skunk!

With happy squeals, Karen and Jonathan jumped to their feet and in two bounds were off the porch onto the lawn. Then they stopped short, their smiles fading.

The skunk was standing stiffly still. Baring its teeth,

it hissed at Sancho. The dog barked in confused little yips. Slowly the skunk raised its tail.

"Wrong skunk!" Karen yelled. "Here, Sancho! Quick, boy!"

Whimpering, the dog turned and ran toward them, and all three dashed onto the porch. On the lawn, the skunk slowly lowered its tail. With a final glance their way, it trotted back into the bushes.

"Whew!" Jonathan said. "If we don't get over thinking that every wild skunk might be Stinker, we're in for a majorly stinky life."

Kneeling down, Karen was patting her shivering dog. "Well, he did say he might come back. It's not our fault all skunks look pretty much alike."

"Yeah," Jonathan said. He gave an angry kick to the porch swing, setting it jiggling. "A lot of things aren't our fault, but they make life stink just the same."

"You can say that again," Karen agreed, rubbing Sancho's ears. "Here two kids who didn't even like each other last year have had the most incredibly cool adventure ever, and bigwigs from NASA and the Pentagon tell everyone it's a lie or a hoax."

Jonathan plunked himself back on the swing. "Right. I mean, the press and TV people were here. They saw all those alien Zarnk with their clattery pole legs. They saw how Stinker and his army of skunks destroyed them with skunk spray. They even saw all the skunks climb into the hijacked space shuttle and take off. And then those government guys don't let the press use any of it after those first live TV shots. They pour on a bunch of garbage, saying it's a hoax and a danger to national security. Give me a break!"

"Well, garbage or not, they managed to convince everyone at school we're a couple of lying trouble-makers."

"That's for sure," Jonathan said, kicking idly at Sancho's chew-bone. "The way other kids treat us now, we might as well have the plague. I mean, it would have been hard enough convincing people that this crash-landed alien took over a skunk body and talked into our minds. But after the government people got through, no one would believe us if we said the sky is blue."

Karen nodded. "And then they had the nerve to question us for hours about what we learned from Stinker—about his weapons and spaceship and stuff. Their cover-up pretty well wrecked our lives, and they still expect us to help them with information we don't even have. And it won't be any better once school starts again next fall. For the rest of our lives, the world will brand us as a couple of lying weirdo freaks."

Angrily, Jonathan stood up and threw Sancho's chew-bone onto the lawn. The dog looked hesitantly into the gathering shadows, then scampered down after it.

"Which just goes to show," Jonathan said, "that life can stink even when you don't have a skunk in it."

1

Presidential Audience

Tsynq Yr's skunk nose twitched nervously. In many ways he was happy with his current body, but just now he would have preferred something more impressive. It was not often that an ordinary Sylon Space Corpsman had a private interview with the president of the Sylon Confederacy. He was scared witless.

With his black-and-white plume of a tail spread proudly behind him, Tsynq Yr hoped he looked confident and dignified. The others in the waiting room ignored him.

He tried to imagine what this meeting would be like. No doubt the president would be full of praise. After all he, Tsynq Yr, had brought back that vital information about the planned Zarnk attack. As a result of that unexpected stop at a little out-of-the-way planet, he had also brought back a shipload of animals that have a natural defense against Zarnk, a disintegrating spray, unknown to the Sylons. Now several colonies of these animals had been set up and were happily reproducing themselves. What a boon they'd be on Sylon worlds near the Zarnk border.

This body of his had been plenty useful while arranging that. Tsynq Yr tried to sit up taller and ignore the Sylon next to him whose current body looked like a huge scaly burrito.

He wondered what the president would look like. The only time he'd seen the president before, at a ceremony, he'd been in the body of an elderly Trith. That had been a while ago, so he'd probably moved into something else by now. What would be a useful body for the leader of one of the biggest interstellar governments in the galaxy?

Tsynq Yr's thoughts jolted to a stop as the receptionist called him. Trying to hold his tail in a confident arch, he waddled into the president's office.

Blinking in the bright bluish light, he looked around the large room. In its center stood an oval desk. Behind it spread a cluster of silver rods like a frozen bush, a "chair" for the creature floating upon it. A Nralshi, Tsynq Yr realized. Not a very practical body for a life of action, but for someone who spends most of the time thinking and giving orders, it was ideal.

"Greetings, Honored President," Tsynq Yr thought toward the chair's filmy occupant.

"Greetings to you, Field Operator Tsynq Yr," came the replying thought. The blue-green draperies floating around the body's core waved gently as if in an ocean current. Then they swirled in slightly, and the glowing core shot its light forward. Tsynq Yr felt himself bathed in a cool blue glow.

"So that is what the remarkable creatures you brought back look like."

"Yes, Excellency. The dominant species on that planet is bipedal while those on the next rung are quadrupedal or aquatic."

Wisps of blue green flicked impatiently. "Yes, yes, I am familiar with the reports. Yours and . . . the others."

"Others?" Tsynq Yr questioned.

"More reports than you can imagine!" The floating draperies trembled angrily. "What am I to do with you? A maverick troublemaker of the first order, it seems. Brilliant, daring, and absolutely disastrous!"

"Uh . . . I don't . . ."

"In one operation you save us from a Zarnk attack and secure a new secret weapon, but at the same time you drag us to the brink of war somewhere else."

"I don't . . ."

"That remote little planet you 'discovered' was in fact well within Twak territory."

"I didn't . . ."

The tendrils tightened, then loosened in a sigh. "I know. You were escaping along the dimensional boundary, lost control, and reappeared there. An accident, but it still was within the Twakish Amalgam."

"I apologize, Excellency, for not understanding the true significance of this, but I've never had much dealings with the Twak."

"That is because the Twak don't want anyone having dealings with them. The Twak are, to say the least, strange. They are eccentric, greedy, reclusive, lazy, and very possessive. What's worse, they are, when they feel like it, very, very dangerous."

The president's filmy extremities had tightened into a dense cloud. "Twakish territory touches ours at several points. The High Gyrn of Twak is now threatening to destroy our border posts if we do not make up for the damage that we—no, that *you* caused."

The president was not the least bit transparent now. He throbbed a solid angry blue.

Tsynq Yr's stubby legs were trembling. "But all I did was . . ."

"All you did was enter Twakish territory without permission, remove several hundred animals from a developing planet, and steal the dominant species' most advanced space vessel. The High Gyrn considers that very close to an act of war. And let me tell you, the Twak may be lazy, but they delight in inventions and they have invented some truly dreadful weapons."

Tsynq Yr's legs gave out totally and he plopped onto the floor. "I . . . I am sorry. I didn't mean to . . ."

With a sigh, the president rippled himself loose again. Blue-green film floated around the chair. "No, your type never means to cause trouble. You do it by instinct. But now you have a chance to get us out of this by instinct. The High Gyrn says that if we don't want our bases destroyed, we can give the same 'creature' who caused this mess the chance to make up for it."

"Meaning me?" Tsynq Yr asked, lying flat and ruglike on the floor.

"Meaning we are sending you to the High Gyrn of Twak for further instructions."

Feeling that already he was as good as eaten and digested, Tsynq Yr dragged himself to his feet and tried to look noble. "Yes, Excellency, I understand. Should I, do you think, change bodies first?"

The president wafted free of the chair and floated around the little skunk, faint streamers trailing behind the glowing core. "No, we don't want to appear threatening, and I cannot imagine a body that appears less threatening than that one. But don't even think of trying that built-in chemical spray on the Twak." Then came a wry laugh. "It probably wouldn't work anyway."

"Understood, Excellency. When am I to leave?"

"Immediately," snapped the reply, as the president swooped back to his chair. "I do have a few other problems in running this Confederacy besides the ones you have created."

Mentally mumbling apologies, Tsynq Yr turned and was scuttling out when a parting presidential thought reached him. "If you live through this, Corpsman, do visit me again. You still are owed some rewards, you know."

As Tsynq Yr hurried through the waiting room he tried not to let his tail drag. But his thoughts were not cheery. "Rewards—oh, right. *If* I live through this. Why did I choose to go into the Space Corps? Think of all the jobs and all the species in the universe. I could have moved into the body of a Bulga gardener and spent a long, happy life tending mushrooms."

Outside the presidential offices he caught a flittership, wrapped his tail around him for comfort, and headed to the spaceport.

2

The High Gym of Twak

From space, the planet Twak was a yellow-orange ball.
There were no oceans, but its surface was gouged by
long green lakes, and here and there Tsynq Yr caught
the glint of a city. As Twak Space Central had instructed,
he left the Earth shuttle he'd been towing in the planet's
orbit and piloted his small Sylon ship toward the capital
city.

During the trip he had been learning what he could
about the Twak. By all accounts they were just plain
odd. They loosely controlled thousands of star systems
but didn't do anything with them except keep outsiders
away, encourage trade among the worlds, and collect
various oddments from them. They didn't get out much,
and left most of their government duties to subject species. The average Twak spent its time thinking, collecting things, and eating. It was the eating part that worried
Tsynq Yr.

At the Twakish spaceport, his ship was met by a peculiar little trolley. It had three round open-air cars—red, yellow, and green—that ran on big blue balloon tires. What pulled it was a jointed mechanical animal with six legs.

Making little tooting sounds, the trolley carried Tsynq Yr past buildings of all shapes and colors. A huge upside-down yellow pyramid towered over a building that looked like a fat green candle with lots of drips. Here and there Tsynq Yr glimpsed what he thought must be Twaks—large wispy lumps of hair.

The trolley took him through tunnels, up ramps, and over bridges until he realized he was now inside some huge building. He rolled through rooms of different shapes and sizes, some empty, some full of things. All sorts of things.

One room was lined with shelves and ledges all holding mechanical devices. Some ticked, some whistled, some flashed, and some tossed balls back and forth. Some seemed to work by steam, others by clockwork, and yet others by antigravity. And none seemed to be doing anything worth doing.

Another room was crammed with statues, big and small, representing all sorts of species. The room next to it held devices that produced what Tsynq Yr guessed was supposed to be music. The clashing mix of different tunes, rhythms, squeaks, booms, and squeals set his fur on edge. After that came a room overflowing with marbles. A force field held these little balls back from the trolley's path in great cliffs, but even so, hundreds of colored spheres rolled and bounced out of their way as the trolley chugged through.

"Eccentric" is hardly the word, Tsynq Yr thought, as they entered a room filled with things that seemed to have nothing at all to do with one another. At the center of the room the trolley suddenly stopped beside a bed of nails, in the middle of which stretched a tangled mass of yellowish white hair. A Twak?

It didn't move, it didn't say anything. Hesitantly, Tsynq Yr stepped from the trolley, which lazily rolled away. Facing the hairy thing, he sat down, wrapped his tail around him, and thought politely, "Hello."

The thought that boomed back into his mind nearly bowled him over. "Hello, hello, hello! Welcome to Twak. Don't have many visitors, you know. Don't *want* many visitors. But you are different, little Sylon. You have got some things to set right, right?"

"Uh, yes. Perhaps I do. May I ask if I have the honor to be addressing the High Gyrn of Twak?"

"You may. Yes, you may."

"Am I?"

"Are you what?"

"Addressing the High Gyrn," Tsynq Yr said, trying to keep calm.

"Indeed you are. What did you think, silly creature? All the others are far too busy with things to bother themselves running this place. That's my job, High Gyrning. Running this bunch of planets—and keeping outsiders from making trouble."

Tsynq Yr cringed at the threatening tone. "I am truly sorry. I didn't mean to make any trouble."

"Why should I bother with what some Sylon did or did not mean? What I am bothered by is what bothers me. People coming where they are not invited and snatching away a shipload of Twakish subjects, that bothers me. For that matter, Sylons bother me, too— can't even decide on your shapes. By the way, is that one of the native animals you're in?"

"Y . . . yes, it is, but I just borrowed it. When I get a chance I could give it back and move into something else."

"No, no, I wouldn't dream of inconveniencing you. And you can keep the others, too. Really quite clever of you to find a spray that wastes Zarnk. If there's one thing I hate worse than Sylon, it's Zarnk. Gross, nasty, mean things."

Tsynq Yr felt his mind spinning. "So you don't mind me taking the skunks after all?"

"Of course I mind, even if it was a smashing good idea. Now you'll just have to make up for it, that's all."

"Uh, yes. How?"

"Well, first, you do have to take back their spaceship. You know, I hardly know a thing about that planet— Earth, is it? It's so far on the fringes, it's really too much of a bother for any of us to visit. Why, we haven't even got anything from there for our collections. Except recordings, of course."

"Recordings?"

"Yes, some years ago they started broadcasting entertainment programs. And jolly entertaining they are, too. Look, here's my library."

The hair ball shrugged sideways and bumped against a console screen. The screen lit up with a rolling list of titles in Earth languages. Tsynq Yr recognized several from seeing them on Karen's TV.

The High Gyrn chuckled to itself and continued. "Very entertaining, indeed, but recordings are not the same as things. You can fill a room with things. You can touch them, you can count them. And I want some thing from Earth."

"Well, why don't you just go there and collect something?"

The creature gave a mental snort. "We like collections, not collecting. We send out collectors, but just now most of our worlds that are into space travel are busy with wars or trade or something. I don't like to bother them. Of course, we've collected enough of their weapon inventions to blow up your border worlds if we choose. But that wouldn't really gain us much, would it?"

"No! No, not a thing."

"Precisely. And it is *things* I so want. So, here's the deal: I won't blow up your bases if you go back to this Earth place, return their little spaceship, and bring me back something."

"What exactly?"

"Oh, a surprise. I love surprises! Of course, it had better be the right surprise."

Tsynq Yr's whiskers twitched nervously. "Any clues as to what that might be?"

"How pushy you are! It has to be something special, something unique, something very Earth. As you can see, I have quite a lot of things already. I wouldn't want any duplicates or same-idea things, would I?"

Tsynq Yr sagged at the thought of all the rooms and rooms of things he had just seen. And that had probably only been a fraction of the collection.

"Come now, it's time you were off," the hairy tangle said, settling comfortably into its spike bed. "All this talk of little Earth has got me hankering to watch one of their shows. I'd invite you to stay but you haven't the time, you know. If I don't hear from you in a bit, I think I will blow up a few of your bases. We've just collected some new weapons that I'm really itching to try."

"And how long is 'a bit'?"

"Until I get tired of waiting, of course. Now do be off."

Abruptly, the little trolley bumped Tsynq Yr from behind. In a daze he climbed in and watched in despair as the thing took him through a new series of rooms bulging with collections.

Once in his ship he wasted no time before taking off, putting a towing beam on the shuttle, and laying course for Earth. Finished with the busywork, he had time to think. And his thoughts were not good.

"Why didn't that creature just eat me or pour melted bronze over me and add me to his collection? It would have saved time. What was that phrase Karen and Jonathan had? 'How on Earth' am I going to do this?"

3

Troubles

On the couch in Jonathan's house, Karen and Jonathan sat with eyes glued to the TV. Occasionally one would dig a hand into the popcorn bowl, scattering a few kernels for Sancho waiting on the rug.

"What you two watching?" Jonathan's father asked as he walked through the room.

"Shh. *Star Raiders Six*," his son said.

"But you've already seen that movie, haven't you?"

"Twice. But this is the first time it's been on TV."

An ad for toilet cleaner came on. Karen, Jonathan, and Sancho padded into the kitchen for a refill on popcorn.

"I still think *Star Raiders Seven* is the best," Karen said. "It's got all that stuff with dragons."

"Nah," Jonathan insisted, "the best is *Star Raiders Three* with the berserk computers. They've all got their good parts though."

"Well, the best part in any of them is the escape from the Spider Swamp in *Four*."

"No, it was the gladiator fight in *Two*. Or maybe the mud flood in *Five*."

"Aren't they ever going to stop making those movies?" his father asked, rummaging in the refrigerator. "That actor who plays the lead Raider must be as old as the hills by now."

"Trevor Conway?" Karen said. "He's not much older than you are."

"Like I said," he laughed, "an old crock. But if I were Trevor Conway, I'd retire with my millions and stop leaping around in front of a camera."

"He can't do that!" Jonathan protested. "No one else can play Alex Greystone, and without Commander Greystone *Star Raiders* is nothing."

"Right," Karen added. "*Star Raiders Nine* is being released this summer, and there are rumors of a *Star Raiders Ten* coming next year. So Conway has to stay on."

Jonathan's father grunted and left the room. "You'd think you two would have had enough of space by now. But at least Greystone and the others are human."

"Lieutenant Cybo is part robot," Karen corrected him.

Jonathan headed back to the TV, yelling over his shoulder, "And my favorite is Zan, the winged Kiptelan."

"But at least there are no skunks," his father called as the screen door banged behind him.

Karen and Jonathan looked at each other, then settled

back to watch the movie. Staring at the screen, Karen said, "Your parents are just like mine. They wish the whole thing last fall had never happened."

"Yeah, but at least they admit it did," Jonathan said, pushing his glasses back along his nose, "not like those NASA people telling the press that they didn't see what they saw."

Angrily, he shook a fistful of popcorn at the TV. Sancho scarfed up the kernels that flew loose. "This sort of stuff isn't just movies. It's really happening out there. Stinker may not look like Commander Greystone, but real adventures happen in space all the time. Those people are just afraid to admit it."

Karen nodded, dipping into the popcorn again. "And having a bit part in one was pretty awesome—when it wasn't totally terrifying."

The movie was almost over when the telephone rang. They were both so involved in the rescue of the rebel priestess by Greystone and Zan that they didn't notice anything else until the credits were rolling. Jonathan's mother was watching them from the living room doorway.

"That was Mr. Blimpton from NASA on the phone. He wants to come here and have another talk with you two."

"Oh, no!" they squealed together.

"There isn't one new question they could possibly ask us," Jonathan complained.

His mother nodded. "That's what I said. But he said they'd been studying the remains of the spaceship and those dead Zarnk creatures, and some more questions have come up."

"Blimpton's the worst of them all," Karen grumbled. "He's like those bad-guy cops on TV. They think if they ask the same stuff over and over you'll break down and confess."

"Do you have something to confess?" Jonathan's mother asked.

"No," said Karen, "but if we did, maybe they'd believe us and leave us alone." She turned to Jonathan. "Let's go outside. Once that NASA creep gets here he'll have us locked up for hours."

The leaves in the woods were the fresh green of early summer, and the birds chirped with special vigor. Karen and Jonathan did not share their mood. Without thinking about it, they walked to the spot in the woods where Stinker's spaceship had crashed and where later they had seen their first Zarnk. The swampy ground was now all torn up from the government people's search for the remains of the Sylon's ship.

"What are they so scared about?" Jonathan asked, as he kicked a rotten log. The smell of rich decay wafted up, then blew away on the breeze. "I mean, pretending there isn't life out there in space isn't going to make us any safer."

"It's crazy, all right," Karen said. "One part of the government digs up the spaceship and tries to figure out how it worked, and another part tells us there aren't any such things as alien spaceships."

Taking a stick, Jonathan began poking around in the log's spongy wood, thinking how Stinker the skunk would have liked eating the fat grubs he was uncovering. The little fellow had liked grubs almost as much as peanut butter. "But if people believed that there couldn't be anything neat out in space, movies like *Star Raiders* wouldn't be such hits."

"So anyway," Karen said, grabbing up a stick and thrusting with it like a laser sword, "let's play Star Raiders. We'll do enough talking once Blimpton gets here. I'll be Alex Greystone."

"You can't be," Jonathan protested, finding his own laser sword. "You're a girl."

"So? 'Alex' can be a girl's name, too. Besides, if you can accept space people who change bodies, why can't you accept a girl being a Star Raiders Commander?"

"Humph. Well, okay. But I get to be Zan. And I carry the disintegrator grenades."

"Right. And Sancho can be that scaly mascot they had in *Star Raiders Two*." She spun around and brandished her laser. "Look out! The Imperials are behind those bushes. We'll have to sneak up on them!"

For hours they stalked, ambushed, and fought their way through the woods. The summer sunshine was now cast by a double star. The leafy trees were strange alien growths, and the soft call of mourning doves was the attack cry of lethal Lubian loons.

They had just worked their way to the edge of the Ice Forest when Jonathan caught a flicker of movement from the corner of his eye.

"There!" Karen yelled. "Use the disintegrator grenades!"

With a fierce cry, he hurled a handful of "grenades."

There was an indignant yelp from behind a bush. Picking a pinecone from his sleeve, Mr. Blimpton of NASA stepped into view.

With his neat gray suit and pale plump face he did look very alien in the sunlit woods. Standing there, he seemed to drain all pleasure from the day.

"Your parents said I might find you here. These alien weapons you were just discussing, are they ones your supposed interstellar friend told you about?"

"Get with it," Jonathan said disgustedly. "They're from *Star Raiders*."

"I bet you never watch those movies, do you?" Karen asked.

"Of course not. They're speculative trash."

"Figures," Karen said, dropping her laser sword and trudging toward home.

For the rest of the afternoon and into the evening, Mr. Blimpton talked with them in Karen's living room. Then, after a brief break for dinner, he turned the tape recorder back on and asked what seemed like the same questions all over again. Once again he had them draw what they remembered of the Sylon power unit. As usual, Karen thought, her drawing looked more like a fat dumbbell with acne. She had just decided to add more knobs at one end when she noticed Jonathan's frozen expression. He was listening to the TV news her father was watching in the next room.

". . . will not confirm these reports. But reliable sources say that this afternoon an unidentified object was tracked moving toward California. Edwards Air

Force Base has been closed to the media, but there are rumors that a vehicle has unexpectedly come down on the landing strip there. One report is that the vehicle is the missing United States space shuttle."

Karen and Jonathan exchanged trembling grins and charged into the TV room. Mr. Blimpton, a look of surprise and worry on his plump face, was following when the phone rang. Karen's mother answered and handed Mr. Blimpton the phone.

"Reportedly," the TV announcer continued, "the vehicle was unmanned and landed according to programmed instructions. Again, none of this has been confirmed by NASA or the air force, but it does lead to speculation that . . ."

Jonathan and Karen, already speculating in one corner of the room, suddenly caught part of Mr. Blimpton's phone conversation.

"I understand, sir. This changes everything. . . . Yes, our only link . . . Yes, I agree, they might have the answers. . . . Is there a flight that soon? . . . Good, you'll arrange it then? . . . Yes, indeed. Good-bye."

Blimpton walked into the room, turning a chummy smile on the two children. "Well, well, you two are in luck. You've just won a free trip to Washington, D.C."

"What?" they chorused.

"Yes, this little business with the space shuttle. All rumors, of course, but it does change things. There are some important people back in Washington who would like to talk with you."

"Now, just one minute," Karen's father objected.

Karen tried to listen to their argument, but in her mind another voice kept butting in.

"Don't do it, kids. I've got a better offer."

She looked at Jonathan and he looked at her. "Did you hear something?" he whispered. She was about to answer when that voice cut into their thoughts again.

"Just pack what you need for a short trip and let's split."

Together they turned and stared out the window behind them. A pointed black-and-white face was peering in, its nose and whiskers pressed against the glass.

"Stinker!" they shouted in their minds.

4

Old Friends

Blimpton and Karen's parents were too busy arguing to notice the kids and Sancho slip out onto the porch. Sancho was so happy to see his old friend that he rolled him over and had nearly bounced him down the steps before Jonathan hauled off the giddy, slobbering dog. With a squeal, Karen swept the skunk up in a big hug.

"Oh, Stinker, we're so happy to see you again!"

The answering thought was a little shaky. "So it seems. But I'm happy to see you, too. It's such a nice quiet planet you've got here."

"We just heard about the space shuttle," Jonathan said. "You programmed it to land in California, then you came here?"

"Right. My ship is in the woods."

Karen glanced back to the house. "You don't suppose radar could have tracked you here, do you?"

"No way. Not this ship."

"Good," Jonathan said. "I think we'd better keep this visit quiet."

Stinker cocked his head. "You had some trouble over the last one?"

Pushing his glasses back, Jonathan sat on the porch railing. "Oh, only over aiding an alien to steal a U.S. government vessel."

"Hey, I just borrowed it. The thing's back safe and sound now."

Karen put Stinker down on the porch swing, out of Sancho's eager reach. "We told them you'd return it. But I think what really freaked all the government people was the idea that there's a universe full of weird-looking aliens with better ships and weapons than we have."

Jonathan nodded, pointing back to the house. "And one of the government guys is in there right now. He wants to take us to Washington and ask a bunch more questions about you and the Zarnk and stuff."

"And you want to go?"

"No way!"

"Good, then here's my offer." Stinker paced back and forth on the swing, setting it jiggling. "I've got to confess, this is not just a social visit. I need your help again. I've been sent on a sort of high-stakes scavenger hunt, and I don't know this planet well enough to have a clue where to start looking."

"Well, what are you looking for?" Jonathan asked.

"I don't know! It's got to be something that would appeal to the High Gyrn of Twak."

"Who?"

"The lunatic who runs this part of space. It turns out that your planet is on the fringes of Twakish territory. And the High Gyrn was really ticked off when I landed here without permission and then went off with a ship-load of native animals. The skunks he says we can keep, but to make up for the act I am to bring back something for his collection."

"So what does he collect?" Karen asked.

"Everything! You should see that place of his. Rooms and rooms of junk from every sort of planet. But he doesn't want just *anything* from here. It has to be something perfect. Something very 'Earth.' And if he doesn't like what I choose, or if I don't bring it back soon enough, he's going to wipe out a bunch of Sylon border bases. It could start a war. Lots of folks could get killed. And all because of me!"

Karen sat down and stroked the white stripe that ran over his head and down his back. "Come on, Stinker, it's not your fault you crashed here, and borrowing the shuttle was the only way for you to get home."

Stinker rubbed gratefully against her hand. "I know. It's not reasonable, but neither is this High Gyrn guy. In fact, he's majorly wacko, as you'd put it."

"What does he look like?" Jonathan asked.

"Hmm. Like that picture you showed me once, of Santa Claus, only without the man."

Karen giggled. "You mean, without the beard."

"No, he's all beard. A great dirty white blob of hair, kind of wispy around the edges. There may be eyes or limbs somewhere, but I never saw any."

"Weird city," Karen commented. "What are . . ."

"Karen, Jonathan," her mother's voice called from inside. "Where are you? We've agreed to let you go to Washington, but that means leaving tonight. You'll have to pack in a hurry."

"What'll we do?" Karen whispered. "We don't want to go with that creep."

Stinker answered, "Go pack, but come with me instead. My ship's in the clearing where we first met. Join me there when you can."

"Karen!" Her mother started to open the door. Stinker dove off the porch into a bush. "There you are. Jonathan, we've already talked with your parents, and they're expecting you home to pack. Mr. Blimpton will come pick you up once Karen is ready."

"Oh, that's okay, I can walk back here."

"Nonsense, young man," Blimpton said from inside the house. "I'll collect you. Your parents were understandably concerned about just sending you off like this, but I'm proud of them and of you. Proud of your good sense and patriotism. This is a grave security matter, and I know you'll want to do everything possible to protect your country from threats—wherever they come from."

"Yeah, sure. So I'll go pack. See you *soon*, Karen."

"Right," Karen said firmly as she hurried upstairs to her room. Grabbing her school backpack from where she'd dumped it the last day of school, she tumbled out the books and began stuffing in some spare clothes.

"You don't have to take your entire wardrobe," her mother called. "Mr. Blimpton says it will only be for a few days."

"Give me a break, Mom!" she yelled back. "I've never been to Washington before. I've got to plan things out."

Karen felt a flush of guilt. She didn't like lying to her parents, but with that NASA guy standing there, what could she do? Grabbing up a piece of Princess of Light notepaper, she scribbled, "Dear Mom and Dad, Stinker returned the shuttle but came here because he needs our help for a few days. Don't worry. We'll be fine. Stinker's a friend. Love, Karen."

Placing the note on her pillow, she slipped out her bedroom door, but instead of going down the stairs she slung on her pack and crept along the hall to the narrow back stairs leading down to the kitchen. No one was about, and she could hear muffled voices coming from the front porch. She had her hand on the knob of the back door when she stopped, tiptoed to a cupboard, and grabbed a bag of peanut butter cookies and a jar of chunky peanut butter. Stuffing these into her pack, she crept outside.

The screen door had just shut behind her when she heard her mother's voice from the front of the house.

"Sancho, no! Come here, Sancho! Good boy!" Her voice lowered. "Did you see that stupid dog? Playing with a skunk! The poor thing thinks every skunk is . . . that one he made friends with."

As Karen quietly headed away from the house, she heard Mr. Blimpton. "A skunk? Maybe it's *the* skunk. That alien thing!"

She was too far away to hear words, but Karen caught the tone of her father's reply, his let's-not-let-our-imaginations-run-away-with-us tone. Giggling, she ran full speed for the woods, only slowing once she reached the sycamore grove. Around her, tall, white tree trunks glimmered palely in the light of the half-moon.

Jonathan had turned down his parents' offer to help him pack, and had rushed upstairs to his room. There he dumped several pocket video games out of a canvas bag and threw in a change of clothes. Now what? He knew his parents would be waiting with hugs and advice near the foot of the stairs. And there wasn't another way down. But what about the emergency escape route he'd planned in case of fire?

He hurried down the hall to the bathroom and threw open the window. Pulling some crumpled paper and a pencil stub from his pocket, he scribbled a note to his parents and stuck it onto the mirror with toothpaste. Then he stood on the toilet and pushed his bag through the window to the short, sloping roof outside. Taking a deep breath, he hoisted himself up and started wriggling out.

The drainpipe, now that he was actually clutching it, felt a lot flimsier than he'd imagined. And the ground looked a lot farther away.

Pretend there's a raging fire behind you, he told himself. Looping the bag handles over one arm, he pushed his glasses firmly back, then gripped the pipe and swung his feet free of the window. The metal creaked alarmingly. The pipe shuddered but held.

Awkwardly, he began climbing down, sure he was making enough noise to alert everyone. His feet clunked against the pipe, and the metal bands holding it to the house screeched in protest. He tried swinging around to the other side. Suddenly, one of the bands popped loose, then another. He scrambled faster, but the top of the pipe buckled outward. There was another screeching pop, and the whole pipe peeled away from the wall. In seeming slow motion it lowered him toward the ground. He tried to keep his grip but his feet flailed loose. Suddenly his hands slipped. He was falling.

5

Not Your Average Trip

With a jarring crash, Jonathan landed on the card table where his mother had set out baby tomato plants. He heard surprised voices from inside but didn't stay to listen. Scrambling up from the litter of dirt, pots, and little green vines, he straightened his glasses, then charged toward the wood. The sound of his feet pounding over the ground made it hard to be sure if someone was calling his name. But someone was yelling something. Too bad he didn't have time to stop and find out what.

Bursting at last into the moonlit grove, Jonathan stumbled to a halt. There it was, the real thing. He could hardly believe it. A real spaceship.

The milky light filtering through the branches washed over the sleek silvery oval crouching on the grass. The only sound in the grove was the steady chirping of insects.

Scarcely daring to breathe in case it vanished, Jonathan stepped forward. His eager glance took in the slanting fin stretching down the back, and the two narrow wings tapering out from the sides. The nose was blunt like the head of a snake. The whole thing was hardly bigger than a large car.

"Shake a leg, Jonathan," Stinker's voice said in his head. "I don't think we made a very clean getaway."

Jonathan shook himself. Over the wind-rustling leaves he could hear voices. He darted toward the dark patch in the ship's side and scrambled up a short ramp into the cabin. No sooner was he inside than the door closed after him and a soft light came on in the small, excitingly alien space.

Karen was already there, looking as thrilled as he felt. Grinning, she said to Stinker, "So where are we going?"

Stinker sat in a small bucket seat by a bank of controls. "Time enough for that later," he answered. "Right now we'd better just go."

He began working the controls. First, the front end of the cabin shimmered and became as clear as glass. Next, a faint ripple of sound and motion swept through the ship. For a second, they could see the trees and bushes of the familiar woods. Then the branches and leaves seemed to come at them, slide past them, and suddenly there was nothing but dark sky and stars.

"We've taken off!" Jonathan gasped. "Just like that!"

"Look!" Karen said, pointing toward the clear wall of the ship as it banked into a wide curve. Below, they could see farm fields, trees, and the lights of two houses separated by a gray strip of road. They could see tiny figures standing on the asphalt, five people and a dog.

"I bet they're looking up at us," Karen whispered. Then she giggled. "A real UFO."

Stinker set the ship to hover, then swiveled around in his seat. "All right, to business. We're on our way, but the question is, where?"

"You expect us to know?" Jonathan asked.

"You're the natives. Think. Where can I find a large number of unusual Earth things in one place? I don't have time to go traipsing all over the planet."

"Sounds like you need a museum," Karen suggested. "But there are trillions of museums here. Every country has bunches of them."

"So where's the biggest and best one?"

"There's a big museum in London," Karen offered. "My grandparents went there once. And what's that one in Paris where they keep all those famous paintings? The Louvre."

Jonathan shook his head. "Hey, no, what we want is the Smithsonian. That's really a bunch of museums all near each other. They've got space stuff, and natural history, and everything. We have a subscription to their magazine."

"Sounds good," Stinker said, "but where is it?"

"In Washington, D.C.," Jonathan answered.

"Hey, is that a good idea?" Karen asked. "That's where those NASA guys want us to go."

"Then that's the last place they'll expect to find you." Stinker chuckled, spinning back to the controls. "Let's go!"

Abruptly, the farm scene dropped away. The moonlit countryside slid silently beneath them.

Once they could tear their eyes away from the view, the two humans looked around the little cabin. There were several other bucket seats like Stinker's but without the controls. The ceiling couldn't have been much over six feet high, and along the back wall were various instruments and gauges. Jonathan put his hand on the smooth portions of wall and felt it trembling slightly.

"Is the engine in the back?" he asked, thinking of all the spaceship models he'd drawn or built over the years.

"Yes. It's a lot more compact than the one in that cheap ship I had last time. This is a top-of-the-line Sylon scout ship. We make all sizes to fit whatever bodies our people might be using. But usually we don't choose bodies much smaller than this one," he said, patting his plump black tummy. "When you're in a body this size, a lot of big lumbering species give you a hard time."

"Well, I'm glad you stuck with it," Karen said. "It suits you." After another moment, watching the dark landscape sweeping beneath them, she said, "Stinker, I hope you have some idea where we're going, because all I know is that Washington is somewhere in the East."

"Hey, remember I read that whole encyclopedia of yours? It had a bunch of maps in it. But I've got to admit they were kind of general. We can find the city all right, but I'm not sure where to go once we're there."

"No sweat," Jonathan said, while watching the rise and fall of some mysterious dials. "We'll just stop off at a corner gas station and buy a map."

"Oh, right!" Karen groaned. Then, rummaging in her

backpack, she pulled out the bag of peanut butter cookies and offered them around. Stinker happily took more than his share. Soon his black-and-white fur was well dusted with crumbs.

Not many minutes later, a glow began smudging the sky ahead. The dark land that had been dotted here and there with clustered lights began to be crossed with ribbons of light like a huge glittering spiderweb.

"Big city coming up," Stinker said. "Washington, D.C.—I hope. Now let's look for that corner gas station."

"Hey, I was kidding!" Jonathan squeaked as they suddenly dropped lower.

"Still need a street map, though," Stinker said. With dizzying speed, they sank down until they were only a few hundred feet above a busy street. "Tell me when you see a likely spot."

Karen and Jonathan both stared out but couldn't focus on anything before it swept by. "Slow down, will you?" Karen said. Instantly, the blur of light became a leisurely passing view of motels, used-car lots, and fast-food places. "There!" she and Jonathan said together, pointing at a familiar gas station sign.

They dropped like a stone onto a motel parking lot beside the station. The door of their ship slid open. "Okay," the skunk said, digging into the nearly empty cookie bag. "One of you go get a good map. Oh, wait, is this one of those places where you need money for things?"

"No problem. I've got some," Jonathan said. Still a little shaken from the suddenness of the landing, he stumbled out, expecting to see a crowd gathered around and pointing at them. But there was only the quiet parking lot and the flashing motel sign. Maybe the whole thing had been so fast nobody had noticed or believed what they saw.

Trying to act as if he arrived in spaceships every day, Jonathan straightened his shoulders, pushed back his glasses, and strode toward the gas station. Minutes later he was walking out clutching a tourist brochure and two maps, one of greater Washington and one of the downtown. An elderly couple was standing beside their ship, gawking.

"This is some car," the man said as Jonathan walked up.

"Yes, isn't it?" Jonathan answered awkwardly.

"Can't say I've ever seen anything quite like it," the man added, stroking his chin. "What's the make?"

"Oh, yes, the make. Well, it's really an experimental model. Not any make exactly. Not yet, I mean."

The woman ran a hand over the glass-smooth surface. "It's very nice and shiny. But isn't it a little large for city driving, for city parking anyway? Goodness, if I had to parallel park this thing, I'd never pass the driver's test."

"Well, it's not really for every day," Jonathan said, praying they'd leave soon, "being an experimental model and all. In fact, we're just taking it to an experimental-car show."

"Well, dear, you're sure to win," the woman said, taking her husband's elbow and trying to steer him away. "It looks just like something out of those space movies our grandsons like, doesn't it, Elmo?"

"Not at all," the man replied as he walked away. "Your

problem, Mildred, is that you don't keep up with these things. All the top companies are showing this sort of design."

Jonathan watched until the two disappeared into their motel room. Then he tapped on the spot where he thought the door should be. It slid open a few feet to his left, and he scrambled in.

"That was wild," Jonathan said as they spread the maps over the floor of the cabin. "An old couple thought this was a regular car."

The little ship smelled of peanuts. Stinker had opened the peanut butter jar and had been sampling. His thoughts came through although his mouth was nearly stuck shut. "Hmm. I wonder if that isn't a good idea?"

"If what isn't a good idea?" Karen asked, taking a crumpled tissue from a pocket and trying to wipe the smudges from peanut buttery skunk paws off the map.

"Acting like this is a car. Street maps are easiest to follow if you're using streets. Even without external lights, someone is bound to notice if we keep flying along several hundred feet above the streets."

"That's right," Karen said, thinking about the UFO-sighting headlines that would get into those grocery store newspapers.

"No way!" Stinker said in response to her thought. "I want to keep this visit low profile. No point in stirring things up on this planet any more than we have. So give me a few minutes to figure out the best route, and in the meantime why don't one of you pop over there and pick us up some more provisions?"

Figuring it was her turn, Karen followed the direction his little nose was pointing and saw a fast-food place with a lit-up sign reading GIANT PEANUT BUTTER MILK SHAKE, 99¢.

"Wouldn't you know!" Jonathan mumbled. "Don't you ever stop eating?"

Stinker sniffed. "I can't help it if this body I borrowed is always hungry. You have to go with the flow, as they say."

Karen shrugged. "I'll go get something. We could probably all use it." After taking everyone's order, she slipped from the ship, checked to see there was no one about, and headed across the dark parking lot to the brightly lit restaurant. Should have used the drive-up window, she thought. Except there was no way to roll down the driver's window on their spaceship.

The closer she got to the restaurant, the more nervous Karen became. Its parking lot seemed to be a hangout for local teens, and kind of tough-looking teens, too.

She felt safer once inside the brightly lit restaurant, with its mixed smells of fried food and disinfectant. Karen placed the order, turned over the money, and received a bucket of chicken nuggets, three bags of fries, and three milk shakes: one chocolate, one strawberry, and one Giant Peanut Butter Special.

Clutching two large sacks, one of hot things and one of cold, she pushed her way out the door. Trying not to see all the older kids lounging around the cars, Karen lowered her head, hurried around the corner, and ran smack into two teenage boys.

"Hey, watch it, kid!" one snapped.

The other broke into a lopsided grin. "Lighten up, Jack. Don't you see this little sweetie is just hurrying to bring us our midnight snack?"

"Why, Bill, how right you are," Jack said, grabbing for one of the bags.

Shrinking back, Karen said, "Sorry, someone else ordered these." She stepped aside, only to find Bill standing in her way.

"Maybe so, but we're the ones who are going to eat them." He reached forward, but Karen ducked away, scared but too angry to give up. She heard Jack and Bill loping along behind her.

A hand gripped her shoulder and spun her around. "Miss, haven't you forgotten our order?"

"Leave me alone!"

"Or you'll do what?" Bill smirked.

"Or I'll . . . I'll call my friends." Looking desperately across the parking lot, her eyes widened in surprise. Jonathan and Stinker were already running toward her.

Catching her expression, Bill looked behind him, then turned back with a sneer. "Those are the friends who're supposed to make us tremble? A little nerd and his lap-dog? Give us a break—and the grub while you're at it."

His friend suddenly gripped his shoulder. "That ain't no lapdog, Bill. I'm out of here!"

"Well, it ain't no Doberman, either," the other jeered. He looked again at the approaching pair. Stinker was walking in a fierce, stiff-legged way with his black-and-white tail held high like a flag.

"Right!" Bill streaked after his friend.

"Thought I picked up a touch of distress," Stinker said into Karen's mind. "Want me to keep after them?"

"No way!" Karen said. "They probably have their whole gang here."

"Besides," Jonathan said, taking one of the sacks from Karen, "if you spray them it will stink up our food."

"Whatever," Stinker said, turning after them and following the delicious-smelling sacks.

Once in the ship, they settled into their seats, divided up the fries and shakes, and plunked the chicken nuggets down between them. Clutching his giant shake with his paws, Stinker took a deep, contented sip. "Ah, peanut butter!" He sighed mentally.

For several minutes the little spaceship was filled with the sounds of munching and slurping. Then Stinker wiped his greasy paws on his fur and, turning back to the instruments, eased the ship out of the parking lot. Hovering a few feet off the ground, it slipped into the sparse late-night traffic.

Dredging one last chicken nugget through the sweet and sour sauce, Jonathan leaned back in his seat and watched the nation's capital flash by. "You know," he said with tired contentment, "this trip isn't half bad."

Giving one last gurgling slurp to her strawberry shake, Karen nodded her head sleepily. "Majorly awesome." Curling up in her seat, she watched the lights slide past them. Neon lights, white streetlights, red and green traffic lights. Red traffic lights? Abruptly, she sat up.

"Stinker, do you know you're supposed to stop at red lights?"

"No. Why?"

"Because there are laws about it!"

Now Jonathan, too, was sitting up, staring out the wraparound window. "Yeah, and there are speed laws, too!"

"Humph," Stinker replied. "Then why aren't the other cars keeping up with those speed laws? Most of them are just poking along—except for those cars with the flashing lights behind us."

"Flashing lights?" both exclaimed. Then Karen asked, "Stinker, are there sirens, too?"

"You want to hear outside noises?" He touched a control and suddenly street sound filled the cabin. Horns blared and brakes squealed as cars swerved to get out of their way. And above that came the not-too-distant wail of police sirens.

Jonathan shuddered. "You know, Stinker, I think your plan for a low-profile visit is kind of shot."

6

Tourists

Karen cringed at the rising sound of police sirens. "We're in big-time trouble if those police stop us. None of us even has a driver's license."

Stinker's thoughts flashed with surprise. "Are those police, the cars with the lights and sirens? Well, no problem. I was just trying to keep our speed down so we wouldn't attract attention."

Karen and Jonathan were thrown back into their seats as the ship suddenly shot forward, dodging through traffic as if everyone else were standing still. Wide-eyed, they watched the monuments of Washington zip by. There were brief glimpses of statues and impressive buildings. One looked briefly like pictures they'd seen of the White House. Then came the lit-up columns and dome of what looked like the Capitol building. Suddenly they careened around a corner and the ship slowed.

"Ah," Stinker said, "this is the area we want. And look, there's some sort of tall fence we can hide behind."

Beside a big modern building they saw that part of the grounds had been walled off by a tall, curtainlike fence. Stinker steered their ship off the road and over the grass. Suddenly they shot up into the air and then down, hopping over the fence like a flea.

On the other side of the tall fence, most of the city lights were screened off. They sat there listening to the distant sirens drawing closer, then, without slowing, going past.

"Whew!" Jonathan said. "Sounds like we lost them."

"Good," Stinker said as he pawed in a greasy paper bag for the last of the french fries. "So let's stay here the rest of the night and get some sleep. Then tomorrow we can do Washington."

"Stinker . . ." Karen began.

"Yes, yes, I know. From now on, it's low profile all the way."

When Jonathan next opened his eyes, he was looking up at a blue morning sky. Birds were chirping. Was he camping in the backyard? He fumbled for his glasses and put them on. There were high wispy clouds in the sky. Beneath the bird song he heard the rumble of traffic. City noise. Then he remembered.

Quickly, he sat up. Karen lay stretched out nearby on the floor of the spaceship, a wadded-up extra shirt as a pillow. Stinker was curled up like a black-and-white cushion in his bucket seat. Suddenly his beady eyes popped open and he raised his head.

"Time to get up and going, is it?"

Jonathan yawned. "Guess so. But what are our plans anyway?"

"My plans are to sleep," came Karen's muffled answer. "So would you two guys pipe down?"

Stinker sat up and shook himself from nose to tail. "What? And miss this glorious morning, this chance to visit your nation's capital. To say nothing of a chance to find what I'm looking for and to—what's your phrase?— get my tail out of the fan? Get my fat out of the fire?"

Karen groaned and sat up. "So where are we going to look for this mysterious something that's going to save your neck?"

"Another good phrase," Stinker commented as he jumped down and waddled toward the map. "This marks all the museums around here, and there're quite a lot. But some look more promising than others."

He sat partway on the map, his furry rump covering large sections of town. With one paw, he pointed to a long green rectangle. "I think we're here. By the"—he squinted at the tiny writing—"by the National Air and Space Museum."

"Fitting," Karen said, scooting herself closer.

"Now right across this green park area, 'the Mall,' there's the National Gallery of Art. North of that is the National Museum of Natural History and north of that is the National Museum of American History. Surely I can find something for that Twakish hair ball in one of those places."

Jonathan frowned. "But if the building we're at already is the Air and Space Museum, why don't we check it out first? That's a place I'd actually *like* to see."

Stinker sniffed. "Jonathan, face it. Your people's puny space efforts are hardly anything to impress the High

Gyrn of a space dominion that includes several thousand stars."

Jonathan shrugged. "I guess not. But after coming all this way, I'd sure like to . . ."

"Okay, we'll fit it in if there's time. Now let's see about some breakfast."

Karen was already doing that, but all she could find were a few broken cookies and about a quarter of a jar of peanut butter. "Guess we'll have to eat out. But I don't have much money."

"Me neither," Jonathan said. "Not enough for fancy restaurants anyway. Maybe for street vendors."

When they stepped out of the ship, however, Jonathan forgot about eating. Their ship was not alone behind the concealing fence.

"Wow! Look at that. It looks almost like . . ."

"Like Alex Greystone's ship in *Star Raiders*!" Karen finished.

In seconds they were across the patch of grass and examining the craft. "It is!" Karen exclaimed. "Look, here's the Star Raiders insignia!"

"And here's a sign," Jonathan said, pointing to a wooden plaque set in the grass in front of the ship. "The *Star Arrow* from the original *Star Raiders* films."

Karen nodded. "I bet that's why this fence is here, so they can hide it until they finish the exhibit or something."

By now Stinker had joined them and was sniffing disdainfully around the ship. "Humph. Poor design, cheap materials. It would never fly. I can't see why you two are so excited about this. My ship's the real thing."

"But so's this," Karen protested. "The real *movie* thing. Trevor Conway and all the other stars have actually touched it!"

"Hmm. Well, do you think we're safe leaving our ship here? Suppose the workers come to do some more setting up?"

"They're not likely to," Jonathan said. "It's Saturday. It should be okay as long as we leave before Monday morning."

"All right," Stinker said, waddling purposefully toward the gate in the fence. "Now let's see to breakfast."

Reluctantly the other two left the *Star Arrow*, but they found the gate locked. "What'll we do now?" Jonathan asked.

"Open it," Stinker said, as he reached into a little compartment in the harness he had strapped around his furry body. "This time I came prepared."

He pulled out something like a stubby pencil and had Karen lift him up to the lock. He touched the two together, and the door swung open.

Cautiously they peered outside. Some distance away they could see a street and people walking along the sidewalk, but no one was near enough to notice the odd group slipping out a door marked MUSEUM PERSONNEL ONLY.

In all directions stretched grass, plazas, and monumental buildings. And scattered about were lots of people.

"You know," Karen said, looking at the skunk, "seeing you could cause a small riot. You'd better ride in my backpack."

"But couldn't you say I was your pet or something?"

"Pet skunks are not everyday things, Stinker. People see a skunk and the first thing they do is freak out. Then maybe they call the police—or the pound. We're trying to keep low profile, remember?"

"But it's so undignified! Suppose I drape myself around your neck like a fur wrap. I've seen pictures of those."

"Skunk fur isn't in style," Karen snapped. "Besides, it's summer. I wouldn't exactly be low profile if I wore a fur wrap in June." She lowered her backpack and opened its flap. "Now, in!"

With a sigh Stinker climbed in, and Karen hoisted the bag on to her shoulders.

"Whew! You've put on a little weight, Stinker. Sure you need breakfast?"

The answering thought was not amused.

They made their way to a street and then crossed it to the Mall, itself a grassy park many blocks long. For the first time they had a good look at Washington, D.C. Above the long green expanse, the sky stretched a glowing blue, crisscrossed by the high white scratches of vapor trails. At one end, set against the blue of the sky, was the marble dome of the Capitol. In the other direction the pale stone needle of the Washington Monument rose from the grass, and beyond it and a long pool of water they could see the white columns of the Lincoln Memorial.

For a while they just stood in the warm morning sun, taking it all in.

"Big, isn't it?" Jonathan said at last.

Karen nodded. "It looks like all those postcards, only for real."

Stinker had been sticking his head out from the top of the backpack. "You people do this monumental thing rather well, I've go to admit."

"How about bringing the High Wack a set of post-cards?" Jonathan suggested.

"That's the High Gyrn of Twak. And no, you do it well, but so do other folks in the universe. I don't think he'd be impressed by pictures of architecture. I, how-ever, would be impressed by a little breakfast."

"With the amount of money we have, it will be a little," Karen said, heading toward a clump of sidewalk ven-dors. They finally selected bean burritos, stuffed one into the backpack, and crossed another wide street to the National Gallery of Art. They stood a moment look-ing up at the marble doorway and pillars, then went inside.

Karen glanced about at all the uniformed guards and shot a mental question at Stinker. "Do you really plan to steal something from here?"

"Not steal," Stinker replied. "I brought along some jewels to leave in place of whatever I take."

"So what do we look for?" Jonathan asked, as he glanced through the tourist brochure. "It says this is one of the largest marble buildings in the world. There must be trillions of paintings in here."

"You just walk. I'll look." Stinker adjusted the top of the backpack so he could see out and not easily be seen.

For hours it seemed, Karen and Jonathan walked up and down stairs and corridors, into big rooms and small ones, looking at paintings, sculpture, drawings, tapestries, and furniture. Their feet were aching and their minds numb before Stinker finally said, "Nope, this isn't the place. On to the next museum!"

"What?" Jonathan exclaimed. "We must have walked twenty miles and seen a zillion dollars' worth of art. Isn't there something your High Quack would like?"

"High Gyrn. Oh, sure, it's all nice enough, but lots of planets produce nice artwork. This has got to be absolutely special or those Sylon outposts will be ashes—along with my career. So what's next?"

Sighing, Karen pulled out the brochure. "Just west of here is the Museum of Natural History. There's got to be something there. But Jonathan, it's your turn to carry the backpack. Some skunks are heavy."

They trudged outside and on toward the building next door. "More marble columns," Jonathan grumbled. "Never knew there were so many in the world." Then he stopped short. "Now, that's more like it."

In front of them was a life-sized statue of a triceratops dinosaur. "How about that?" Karen suggested.

Stinker snorted. "Nothing new. I went to a ball once where the hostess looked a lot like that."

Inside, they found stuffed wild animals from every continent and fossils from every age, but Stinker remained unimpressed. "Hey, look," he said, when the others persisted, "the universe is full of funny-looking creatures. Some are just animals and some can make spaceships, but one more is not going to excite the High Gyrn."

"Jewels, then," Karen suggested. "There are galleries full of diamonds and emeralds and stuff."

"Small change," Stinker sniffed. "We've got machines that can turn out dozens of those in a minute."

"Well, why don't—" Jonathan was interrupted by a woman's scream.

"Guards! Those children have a live animal in that pack. I saw it move!"

"Hey, now, kids," a bulky guard said, stepping up to them. "No pets allowed in here, you know."

"Pets?" Jonathan blurted. "Oh, no, she's mistaken, sir. I haven't got any pets."

"Well, let's just see, shall we?" the guard said with a tired smile.

"Oh. Ha, ha, pets. Of course!" Karen said suddenly. "She must have seen my toy, my *stuffed* skunk. I just bought it. It's really cute, and *stiff* like a toy you know."

"Really?" the guard said, cautiously peering into the top of the backpack. He reached in and slowly pulled out a plump, glassy-eyed skunk, its legs stiff as sticks. Under its fur were glimpses of a blue, plastic-looking harness.

"Sorry, lady," he said with a chuckle. "It's a toy, all right. Cute, don't you think?"

"I do not! I think it's disgusting. A toy skunk, of all things! How vile!" As she stomped away, Karen caught a flicker of thought about what a certain skunk would like to do to her.

"You know, I wouldn't mind having one of these for my own kid," the guard said, poking Stinker's tummy. Where'd you get him?"

Karen's mind buzzed with Stinker's thoughts. "Make him put me back! If I don't blink, breathe, and wiggle soon, I'll explode!"

"Oh, we got him at a toy store yesterday," she told the guard. "Sorry I don't remember where. But we have to go now."

"Sure," the guard said, giving Stinker's tail one final ruffle, then stuffing him back in the bag. "But thanks for the chance to put one of those bossy biddies in their place. Made my day."

Jonathan felt the backpack thump and wiggle as they hurried for the door. "How humiliating!" came the thoughts. "Me, a crack Sylon pilot, having to act like a cute fuzzy toy!"

"Then keep your cute fuzzy head out of sight," Jonathan muttered.

It was midafternoon when they stood outside again. "Where next?" Jonathan asked with a discouraged sigh. He shoved his glasses back along his nose.

Karen pulled the crumpled brochure from a pocket. "The Museum of American History?"

"Right," Stinker replied. "But after lunch."

"We haven't got enough money for lunch."

"I'll waste away! I'll starve!"

"Not likely," Jonathan snorted. He felt a kick from the backpack. "Here, Karen, it's your turn to carry this."

As they transferred the pack, Karen said, "Look,

there's a guy selling pretzels. Maybe we have enough for one of those."

Minutes later they were sitting on a bench, dividing a big soft pretzel three ways. Wearily, they chewed and watched the tourists bustling past. Several kids with dinosaur balloons galloped by, then came a woman pushing a stroller. The toddler in it was waving a large sugar cookie and chanting to itself. As the woman stopped to read a map, Karen felt the backpack buck. There was a streak of black and white, and suddenly the baby was looking wide eyed at its empty hand.

"Doggie!" it announced. "Doggie like cookie."

The woman looked up, stared a minute, then screamed.

People turned their way. "Look, Daddy," a little boy cried, pointing under the bench. "A kitty!"

"A skunk!" someone else yelled. "Call the police! Call the pound! Help!"

7

Something Very Earth

Jonathan sprang to his feet, and Karen squatted down so Stinker could jump into the backpack. People were screaming and pointing, and one of the children with dinosaur balloons was charging their way.

"Neat! A real skunk. Let's see!"

The boy's balloon popped on the handle of the stroller. The baby screamed, and Stinker took off like a black-and-white rocket.

"Guns! They've got guns like on TV!"

"No, Stinker! It's a balloon. Wait!" Karen thought back as she and Jonathan ran after him.

The sight of the galloping skunk set more people screaming, and by the time they'd reached the trees and bushes around the next building, they thought they could hear a police siren as well.

"Why didn't I come back in a different body?" Stinker's thoughts wailed from somewhere deep in the bushes. "Something that could command a little respect around here. Something like that triceratops of yours."

"No way I'd carry *that* in a backpack," Jonathan said. "Though I bet even a triceratops couldn't get us in as much trouble as a greedy skunk. Now, come out and get in this pack."

"Humph. I ought to give them all a good spray for scaring me like that."

"That's the last thing we need," Karen said. "Then they'd come with real guns." She turned around and saw a police officer trotting up to them. "They already have. Get inside!"

She stuffed the pack deep into the bushes. Branches rustled, and the pack jumped about. In one swoop she yanked it out and flung it onto her back.

"Hey, kids," the police officer said behind them. "If there really is a skunk around here, you'd better stay clear. It might be rabid."

"Oh. Right," Jonathan said. "We just wanted to see it. You know, scientific interest and all."

"It was probably just a cat anyway," Karen added as they hurried away.

The next museum was square and modern looking, but they were in such a hurry to get out of sight they didn't notice much of anything until they were inside. A large, tattered American flag was hanging on the wall. Jonathan glanced at the label and said, "Don't even think about taking this, Stinker. It's the original Star-Spangled Banner."

Stinker was going to make snide comments about collecting old rags, but when he picked up the thoughts of the other two he decided against it. "Let's check out something else."

They did. For hours.

"How about this statue of George Washington in a toga?"

"Too big."

"This dollhouse made for President Cleveland's kids is pretty neat."

"I"ve been on planets where the real houses are that size."

"I don't suppose the High Twak would want the gown worn by Mrs. Lincoln at their inaugural ball?"

"You guessed it."

For a while, thinking back on all the gadgets in the Twakish collection, Stinker was tempted by a model steam engine, a sewing machine, and a clock with mechanical figures from American history. But finally he gave up those ideas.

"Anyone who's got that many gadgets is bound to have things that are almost the same," Stinker griped, as they headed out of yet another exhibit gallery. "What'll I do? That loony hair ball is going to start an interstellar war, all because I can't find the perfect souvenir."

"Hey, don't give up," Karen said, feeling very much like giving up. "There are still lots of museums left. We can eat at soup kitchens and keep looking until you find it."

"Great," Jonathan muttered, pushing at his glasses. "Days and days of marble buildings and glass cases. It wouldn't be so bad if we could stop and actually *look* at this stuff. Some of it's pretty cool." He sighed. "At least when people are looking for a needle in a haystack, they know what a needle is supposed to look like."

They continued bickering, trudging through another gallery with Stinker staring half asleep from under the flap of the backpack.

"Stop!" he suddenly thought at them.

Karen and Jonathan stopped dead, staring fearfully around. No guards. No pointing children. No screaming ladies.

"Back there. That exhibit!"

Jonathan looked back at the sign. "It's about enter-tainment—old movies and TV. Hey, if you didn't want that old telegraph machine, why should you want an old movie projector?"

"Just let's go look, okay?"

Sighing, they changed directions and walked through the exhibit. Among photos of old-time stars, there was furniture used on an old TV show, the red sweater once worn by TV's Mr. Rogers, and some famous musicians' piano. Music drew them on. It was a recording of Judy Garland singing "Somewhere over the Rainbow." There were life-sized photos of Dorothy, the Scarecrow, the Tinman, and the Cowardly Lion all skipping down the yellow-brick road to Oz.

"Somewhere over the rainbow," Karen muttered. "That's about the only place we'll find this special thing." Then her mind fizzed with Stinker's mental shriek.

"That's it! There! I've found it!"

"What? Where?" Karen and Jonathan asked, turning around.

"Those shoes!"

They looked at a small, clear case holding two sparkly red shoes. "Dorothy's Ruby Slippers?" Karen asked in surprise.

"Yes, they're perfect! The only thing the High Gyrn has from Earth is your TV transmissions. He's a real old-movie buff. He showed me his catalogue."

"And he's seen *The Wizard of Oz*?" Karen asked.

"Yes! Even I saw it when I was with you before. It's a classic. No other people in the universe would have made a story quite like it, and no other place in the universe would have Dorothy's original Ruby Slippers."

"Okay," Jonathan said, "go for it. But that case'll be sealed."

"Hey, give me a break. There's a laser gun in my harness pocket. It'll cut through anything."

Pretending to be interested in a nearby exhibit, Karen and Jonathan waited until there were no other visitors in that area. Then they lifted Stinker out of the backpack and plunked him down beside the case. He was clutching a flat red triangle in one paw. They turned around and stood like a screen, talking, to hide the faint sound of something being cut.

Then they heard a tiny clink.

"Done!" came the mental message. "I've got the top off. Now I'll just climb inside and hoist out the shoes."

They talked louder to hide the scrabbling sounds and the two thumps. "Think two diamonds are enough in trade?"

"Yeah, that's plenty," Jonathan said. "But hurry up, there're some people coming."

"Drat. Now I'm stuck. Help me out, will you?"

Turning around, Jonathan reached into the lidless case, pulled out the fat little skunk, and put him into the pack on Karen's back. They had each picked up one of the slippers when a voice called, "Hey, you kids, what are you doing?"

"Us?" Jonathan squeaked, spinning around and staring at the guard. "Uh . . . nothing. Just . . ."

"Running," Karen added, as she turned and sped toward a door. Jonathan was right behind. Their minds were hit by Sylon curses as Stinker was jolted up and down in the pack.

Behind them there was shouting and the piercing squeal of a whistle. They pelted down a hall with the sound of shouts and footsteps close behind. Now a siren was screeching through the building. They ran up one staircase, along a hall, and down another staircase. More footsteps and shouting. For a moment their pursuers were slowed when Stinker thrust his hind end out of the jolting backpack and let loose a cloud of stinging, gagging stench.

There was a door ahead of them. One guard even had a gun, but they barreled past him and burst into the open air.

In front of them stood three men: a police officer, a man whose uniform patch said ANIMAL SHELTER, and NASA's Mr. Blimpton.

8

Take Me to Your Leader

A broad smile spread across Mr. Blimpton's even broader face. "Well, well. Am I good at this or what?"

"What?" Jonathan panted.

"I'd just gotten back into town and, on a hunch, put out a request for information on unusual skunk sightings anywhere in the country. And what should come through on the police radio right here in town? A crazed skunk on the Mall. Now here I am, and here you are."

"Wrong!" Karen yelled. Grabbing an ice-cream cone from a startled bystander, she squashed it into Blimpton's face as she and Jonathan barged past him.

They dodged along a sidewalk crowded with tourists. Ahead was an even denser clump, children waiting to file onto a big yellow bus. They swerved around it and came across another group that had almost finished loading into a second bus.

"Camouflage," Jonathan called to Karen as he skidded

to a halt at the end of the line. The kid ahead of them looked at the newcomers.

"Boy, that was close," Jonathan panted, straightening his glasses. "Thought we were going to miss the bus."

It was their turn. They crowded up the bus stairs. A flustered woman was trying to deal with someone's lost spending money and didn't glance at them. They looked back into the noisy bus and crammed into a seat beside a plump girl with pigtails.

"Hi, I'm Tess," the girl bubbled. "I bet you're from Miss Morton's group. Don't you want to ride on your own bus?"

"Nah," Jonathan said.

The bus doors folded closed, the engine grumbled, and they began to pull away from the curb.

Karen looked nervously out the window, then added, "There were some bullies bugging us on the other bus, so we're taking this one."

"Smart. I hate bullies. Hey, weren't those museums neat? The ball gowns were totally awesome. But I think I liked the animal and fossil museum best. I got something totally cool at the gift shop."

Karen was listening to Stinker's complaints about being squished, so she sat forward in her seat trying not to lean on the backpack.

Jonathan answered the girl. "Oh, what?"

"This." She reached into a bag and pulled out a hot-pink plastic windup dinosaur. "When I turn this it walks, and opens and closes it mouth. My mom gave me ten dollars to spend. Did you get anything?"

Jonathan smiled. "Yeah. I got a windup stuffed skunk."

"Don't you dare!" came the shout in his mind.

"But I left it with Miss Morton for safekeeping," Jonathan finished.

Karen, peering out the window, glimpsed four men who were looking at the kids on the sidewalk, and then starting to run after their bus. The bus picked up speed and turned a corner.

"I wonder how long this trip will take?" Jonathan asked, wondering really if it would take them to Georgia or somewhere else they didn't want to go.

"Only a few minutes, I guess," said their seatmate. "Miss Campbell said the White House is really close."

"Oh. Right," Karen said. In her mind Stinker was saying, "Good. Then we can get off there, head back to the ship, and cut out of here."

A few minutes later the bus pulled up beside a white building surrounded by an iron fence. Jostling and jabbering, everyone filed off the bus. Karen and Jonathan started to head down the sidewalk, but a woman turned them around and in a stern voice said, "Other way, dears. We're already late so let's go right in, shall we?"

Before they knew it, they were swept in with the other kids through an unimpressive little side door. A guide was saying, "Welcome to the White House, home of the nation's presidents. Move this way, please."

"What do we do now?" Karen whispered.

"I guess this is as good a place to hide as any," Jonathan whispered back.

"Yeah, but I think those guys may have figured we got on the bus."

"Think they can pick us out among all these other kids?"

"They can pick out my turquoise-and-pink backpack."

"Which you are not dumping," Stinker added in their minds. "Have you got the Ruby Slippers safe?"

They both patted bulges in their windbreakers and told him they had.

"Good. Then head for the first exit you find. I don't want to keep the High Gyrn waiting much longer."

They worked their way to the edge of the crowd following their guide. Then, when she was pointing out some dishes in a china cabinet, they slipped into the tour group just ahead of them. Moving from group to group, they had already gone up one flight of stairs and were just leaving a long glittery gold room when Karen glimpsed the animal shelter man entering at the other end. They rushed through the Green Room, the Blue Room, and the Red Room, explaining to disapproving guides that they had fallen behind their group.

"Someday," Karen whispered, "I'd like to really take a look at this stuff."

Jonathan whispered back, "Someday when we aren't carrying stolen property and a furry space alien."

In the elegant State Dining Room they were trapped for a moment behind a large group of wide people, staring at the glistening china and chandeliers. Finally they wormed their way through to a long marble hall with a red carpet, a staircase going up, and, best of all, an open door going out.

They were just heading toward it when they heard a jingling and barking. A floppy-eared black dog came galloping down the stairs. Behind him a young woman was calling, "Bubba, come back here!"

Bubba happily pushed himself through the crowd of tourists, wagging his tail and receiving pats. Smiling with the others at the dog's antics, Karen and Jonathan skirted the group and stepped toward the door.

Just then Bubba stopped, growled, then started barking. Barking at Karen. Karen backed away, but the dog bounded forward, barking and making little half jumps.

"Bubba! What's gotten into you?" the woman cried. "Leave that girl alone!"

The dog continued forward. Then, as Karen turned to run, he leaped up and smacked both paws into the backpack.

A ball of black-and-white fur shot out of the pack like a cannonball. It landed with a thud on the red carpet and started running. Yapping happily, Bubba took up the chase.

"Where's the door?" Stinker squealed. But he saw only legs, legs of screaming people dodging every which way. Suddenly there was a stairway. The red carpet spilling down it was empty. Stinker shot up it, a black-and-white streak, with the snarling dog close behind.

At the top of the stairs, more people. He charged down a hall. To get away from the snapping jaws he leaped onto a small table. Skidding along the marble top, he knocked off a china vase and shot right off the edge.

Dizzily shaking his head, he saw only more doors and hallway. No escape there. Behind him, someone lunged for the dog and caught him. Stinker spun around and charged back down the hall the way he had come. As the skunk passed the frantic dog, Bubba pulled himself free and resumed the chase.

Stinker glimpsed Karen and Jonathan almost at the top of the stairs. A guard yelled from below that the public wasn't allowed up there. The dog was nearly on him. Just then a man stepped out of a doorway. A tall man. Stinker ran right up his front and perched panting on his shoulder. His tail splayed across the man's face.

"Mr. President, watch out!" a voice called.

"Watch what? All I see is black-and-white fur."

"Hold very still, Mr. President," ordered another voice. "We can shoot it off."

"No! Someone just hold that dog, and I'll get it off." Brushing away the tail, the president tried to look at the creature clinging to his shoulder. "Nice kitty. It's all right. Bubba won't hurt you."

"Greetings, Sir," Stinker said clearly into his mind. "I am sorry I don't have time to open proper diplomatic relations. But I've got to go. Top secret business, you know."

With a flip of his tail, Stinker sprang for the banister, and gripping all four legs around it, he slid down. Karen and Jonathan shrugged, smiled feebly at the president, and ran back down the stairs.

"Someone shoot that skunk!" a man called.

"Skunk?" the president said. "No, wait. Don't shoot it!"

The security man lowered his gun. "Why not, sir?"

"I've got an odd feeling about that skunk."

"What do you mean, sir?"

"It's . . . uh, top secret."

9

A Tale of Two Ships

The tourists milling around the open door parted like the Red Sea as the skunk raced through them, followed by two running children. Outside, in the drive, a gray limousine had just pulled up. A uniformed doorman opened the door to let out an impressive-looking gentleman in colorful robes.

Without a pause, Stinker bounded past the visitor and over the seat into the front. The driver took one look at his new passenger and bolted out his door, leaving the limousine in the possession of one skunk and two young humans.

"Good, the engine's still running," Stinker said. "Now you two get up here. I'm going to need help driving this thing. It's not made for a pilot my size."

As Jonathan and Karen clambered over the seat into the front, they could see several men running toward the car. Karen hit a button marked Door Lock, and the locks on all the doors clicked down at once.

"Quick, how do you make it move?" Stinker squealed in their minds.

"Press one of the pedals," Jonathan said, sliding into the driver's seat and putting Stinker on his lap. He stretched his legs far down and pressed one pedal, then the other. Nothing happened.

"You've got to shift the gears," Karen yelled, grabbing a lever and jiggling it. The car leaped backward and the men hammering on the doors reeled back.

Frantically, Karen shifted the lever again. The car shuddered, then shot forward.

"Guess I found the right pedal anyway," Jonathan said, boosting Stinker up so he could see over the dashboard. The little skunk gripped the wheel with two paws and the limo wove wildly down the White House drive.

"It's a little different from flying a spaceship, but I'll catch on," Stinker said excitedly.

"Better hurry up about it before we total this thing!" Karen cried, struggling to get her seat belt on.

"Faster!" Stinker ordered. "I think I've got the hang of things now."

Jonathan scrunched down so he could press the gas pedal harder. Stinker scrambled onto his shoulder.

"Hey," Jonathan complained, "now I'm so low I can't see much."

"You're lucky!" Karen said, watching in horror as the limo dodged through traffic, causing cars to swerve and pedestrians to scatter. Over the blasting horns and squealing brakes rose the sound of sirens.

"They're after us," Karen said, craning around to

stare out the back window, "and we don't have a super-fast spaceship this time."

"It's okay," Stinker assured her. "We've got a head start and all we have to do is get to the space museum, dive into my ship, and take off. No sweat, as you say."

"But not as I do," Jonathan muttered, feeling the sweat prickling out all over him.

"Sounds like an army of sirens," Karen said, craning around again.

"Why not?" Jonathan said, while trying to keep Stinker's tail out of his mouth. "There should be the police from the park, Blimpton from NASA, the animal control guy, a Smithsonian guard or two, and no doubt lots of Secret Service officers from the White House. I wonder why the CIA, the Pentagon, and the FBI haven't gotten into the act?"

"Are you being funny?" Stinker asked, while swerving around an ice-cream truck.

"Yeah, but I'm not laughing much."

Suddenly Karen recognized places. "Hey, we're almost there. But what's that big crowd?"

Ahead, outside one end of the Air and Space Museum, a large crowd was gathered on plaza and lawn.

"Isn't that where we hid the ship?" Jonathan asked, struggling to get up high enough to see.

"I'm not sure 'hide' is the right verb anymore," Stinker said as he steered the limousine toward the curb. "Change pedals, please."

Jonathan jammed down the other pedal as well, and the car shuddered into an odd, grinding squeal. Quickly

• 69 •

he shifted to the brake pedal only, and they stopped so suddenly that Stinker flipped forward and would have smashed into the windshield if he hadn't been clutching the steering wheel so hard. Lying upside down on the dashboard he said, "Not the smoothest landing, but we're here."

They opened the doors, and with the sound of sirens shrieking closer, they got out and plunged into the crowd. People were so tightly packed most didn't notice the skunk running between their feet, though they weren't too happy about the two kids forcing their way through. When the fugitives reached the front of the crowd, though, they stumbled to a halt.

The fence that had so conveniently hidden the spaceship had been pulled back. On the grass, in plain view, the little Sylon scout ship sat next to the movie model. A man in a shiny costume stood behind a podium speaking to the crowd.

Karen and Jonathan both recognized him at the same time. "Trevor Conway!"

"As I said," the actor's familiar voice boomed over the microphone, "this is an age of surprises. The gift of this famous Star Raiders model is a surprise for the American public. The second model, I must admit, is a surprise to me. But Hollywood studio people are like that. Always keeping you a little off balance so you stay on your toes."

The crowd laughed.

"But I suddenly realized that it's meant to be a *happy* surprise for both of us. This other ship, with its bold new lines, can be none other than the model designed for *Star Raiders Ten!*" The crowd cheered. "Which means that speculation in the media can finally end. There *will* be another *Star Raiders* movie!" The crowd cheered more wildly. "And because they chose *me* to reveal this, it must mean that speculation about my own career can also end. The studio must mean for Trevor Conway to return as Alex Greystone and to blast through the universe once again!" The crowd went totally crazy.

"Sorry to disappoint him," Stinker muttered mentally, "but it's time we did our own blasting through the universe." He began trotting briskly across the grass toward his waiting ship.

Karen and Jonathan had started to follow when the crowd around them was forced aside by several men. They both bolted forward, but men lunged and gripped their arms.

"Got them!" someone said.

"Good. Anyone seen the skunk?"

Several people in the crowd were now screaming and pointing to where a skunk loped across the grass.

"There!" a man beside Karen yelled. As someone else yanked her away, she saw the man raise a rifle.

"No! You can't!" she screamed.

The gun popped like a balloon.

Twenty feet away, Stinker flipped through the air and lay still, a small black-and-white lump on the green grass.

New Directions

"Stinker!" Karen cried, but no familiar voice touched her mind. She and Jonathan were steered roughly back through the crowd. Once on the sidewalk, a new, smaller crowd surrounded them, all looking grim.

A police officer stepped up. "Thank you, gentlemen. I think I can take charge from here."

"Afraid not, officer," Mr. Blimpton said, flashing some identification card. "This is a top secret national security matter."

The police officer grunted but stepped back, only to have a museum guard push his way forward. "Security or not, there is still the matter of stolen museum property." He stared down at the two children. "Where are the Ruby Slippers?" Both Karen and Jonathan put hands in pockets, and each pulled out a sequin-covered red shoe.

"They were bought, not stolen," Jonathan said sullenly.

"But they're no use now," Karen said, feeling too numb to be very angry. "Take the miserable things."

In a confused swirl of people, they were hustled into a waiting car. It sped off with Karen, Jonathan, and Blimpton in the backseat. The two children stared blankly out the windows at the Washington street scenes.

"Quite a chase you led us," Blimpton said. They both just sat there.

"You can wait until you get to my office before you talk about this, if you want."

After another long silence, Jonathan said, "I don't think I *want* to talk about it. I want to go home."

"Yes, in time, but you have a great deal to tell us first."

"Wrong," Karen said coolly. "I wouldn't tell you if your coat was on fire."

They spent the rest of the ride in stony silence.

Outside the museum, the animal control officers apologized for the interruption and hurriedly scooped the skunk body into a carrying cage. They made their way through the crowd and slid the cage into the back of their truck, setting off a chorus of barking from the two dogs already caged there. Ignoring the noise, they walked around the truck, climbed into the cab, and drove off.

"Well," the driver said, "that was one of the weirder assignments in my career."

His companion nodded. "In this town, you learn not to ask questions, but I've still got plenty."

"Yeah, like why we got last-minute orders to use tranquilizer darts instead of bullets, and then why we're supposed to bring this skunk to the Pentagon. Why should the military care about some displaced skunk?"

The other shrugged. "Beats me. But I sure don't want to be around when that little wood pussy wakes up."

"We won't be. That stuff will last an hour at least."

In the back of the truck, however, a stubborn Sylon mind was already struggling against a sleepy skunk body. Moments later, beady black eyes popped open. Dizzily, Stinker struggled to his feet.

He felt around with his mind and found the two dog minds filled mainly with anger at being cooped up. He reached further, probing into the minds of the two humans in the cab. He was being taken to a place called the Pentagon, the headquarters for this nation's military. Bad idea.

Quickly he reached through the bars of the cage and twisted open the lock. Wonderful, he thought, what clever skunk paws can do with a clever Sylon mind behind them.

Jumping out, he waddled to the Saint Bernard's cage and opened it, doing the same for the gray mutt next to him. Then he jumped back into his own open cage and hissed at them both. They barked, pushed against their cage doors, and burst out. Stinker hissed and taunted. The dogs broke into a frenzy of barking and growling, but couldn't get at the skunk—and knew enough not to try too hard.

"What on Earth is going on back there?" the driver asked. "I bet one of those mutts got a paw caught again. Told them we need new cages. Better check."

He parked the truck and his partner got out, walked

around back, and opened the door. The two big dogs looked at him for a split second, then bowled him over onto the sidewalk and tore down the street. He was just struggling up when a skunk landed with all four feet right on his stomach, hopped off, and disappeared into some bushes.

"This has been an outstandingly bad day," the man said, staring up at the early evening sky.

It was dark when a tired, bedraggled skunk finished his trek through the alleys and parks of Washington back to the Air and Space Museum. The crowd was gone. Around the outdoor exhibit stretched a new fence. Its gate was open. His tail drooping with exhaustion, Stinker plodded toward his ship, then froze in its shadow. A man was standing there. The man in the unusual shiny outfit. The man Karen and Jonathan had called Trevor Conway.

He just stood there looking at the sleek silver ship. Stinker was about to peek into the man's mind when another man came up behind the first and clapped a hand on his shoulder.

"So there you are, Trevor. Come on back to the reception. These Smithsonian people are really going all out. They may be cool space-science types, but one real movie star has turned them all to jelly."

The other snorted. "Like one real spaceship would turn me to jelly. But you know, Vince, with this model it's somehow not so hard to pretend. It's a real beauty, isn't it?"

"Guess so. And a surprise all right."

"You mean, you didn't know about it either?" Conway asked.

"Oh, you know those guys at the studio, always teasing you along."

"Well, it hasn't been very funny lately. I don't mind telling you, Vince, I've been scared. Scared there wasn't going to be a *Star Raiders Ten*, or if there were, scared I wouldn't be cast in it. Too old, like some of the magazines are saying."

"Nonsense, Trevor. Those are just rumors. Besides, even if they did let you go, it wouldn't be the end of the world. You're a world-famous actor. You could get any part you want."

The actor shook his head. "That's the problem. There's no other part I really want. I'm being unprofessional, I know, but *Star Raiders* has become more than a job for me. It's a dream. As Alex Greystone I get to bring that dream to millions of people all over the world. But I get to live that dream a little myself."

The other barked out a nervous laugh. "Sure. As the actor who plays Alex Greystone you get treated like royalty. Look at that lifetime NASA pass. It can get you in to watch shuttle launches whenever you want."

"I don't think you get it, Vince. It's not the celebrity bit I mean, and I hate those launches—because it's not *me* in those little ships. As Alex Greystone I can make generations of kids dream about going into space, and some of them will do it. But never me! All I have is the dream."

"And a major acting career."

"Vince, face it, my career is winding down. A few more movies at best, and I'm finished. What else do I have? I have no family. I have nothing except this dream of a universe I'll never see."

"Trevor, aren't you a little old to act like a moody artist? You're a big star, for crying out loud! Come on back in and act like one."

Conway laughed. "Hey, doesn't my age even allow me to be philosophical? Okay, I'll be right in. But let me dream over this ship a couple of minutes more before I see it close up in the daylight and notice it's only painted plywood."

As Vince walked away, the actor rubbed an appreciative hand over the slick metal surface. He traced a finger along one tapering fin and tapped the side, listening to the chimelike ring.

Then he laughed and said to himself, "Get a grip, Trevor, old boy. You're checking this baby out like something in a new-car showroom."

Mentally clearing his throat, Stinker stepped out from the shadow of the ship. "Hey, mister," he said into Conway's mind, "have I got a deal for you!"

The actor spun around. The look on his face was like the one he'd had in *Star Raiders Four* when Alex Greystone saw the jelly beast rise out of the sinkhole.

11

Like in the Movies

They had been in that office for hours. Men and women in suits and uniforms had questioned them. Jonathan and Karen had said nothing. It had taken only a whispered exchange in a hallway for them to agree. They would tell these people nothing at all. Why should they? If it hadn't been for them, Stinker would be alive. He'd be off in his sleek silver ship. He'd have the Ruby Slippers, and he'd save his people from war. But now that was all over. These murdering meddlers didn't deserve to learn a thing.

Of course, Karen thought, as she sat in front of a desk ignoring another avalanche of questions, it would almost serve them right to learn how they'd really messed up things. Except that they wouldn't believe it. Sure, a wacky hair ball space emperor wants Dorothy's Ruby Slippers or he'll beat up on a bunch of body-hopping space people. They'd never get it, particularly since the source had been a skunk. There'd be another cover-up, and if the two of them ever tried to tell the truth, they'd be branded as worse freaks than before.

Someone asked if they were hungry. She supposed she was. She didn't feel much of anything. After a bit, some sandwiches were brought in. Karen took one look at hers and burst into tears. Peanut butter.

"Well, I can see you're both tired," Mr. Blimpton said awkwardly. For the moment he was the only questioner left in the room. "So let's call it a night, shall we? There're a couple of hotel rooms booked for you, and we can talk more in the morning."

"Not in the morning, not ever," Jonathan said. "We want to go home. Now."

"Don't be absurd, children," Blimpton snapped, walking to the door. "There's a lot we have to discuss yet— once you're rested. Your parents have been called. They know you are safe and will be staying with us for a few days."

"Hey, don't we have some sort of rights?" Jonathan objected, angrily pushing back his glasses.

The only answer was a smile as Blimpton whisked them out of the room into a hallway.

"If only we still had the Ruby Slippers," Karen whispered, "we could try clicking them together."

"Anything'd be worth a try," Jonathan muttered.

They started walking down the hall when they saw someone coming their way. Karen grabbed Jonathan's arm. "Hey, isn't that . . . ?"

"Yeah, it is. And in full uniform, too."

Trevor Conway, the actor, strode confidently toward them. "Why, Mr. Blimpton! Nice to see you again. We met at the last shuttle launch. Since I was in town, I thought I'd take advantage of my NASA pass and come visit your establishment here."

"Ah, yes. Mr. Conway, we're honored. It is a little late, but once I take care of these two young people I'll be happy to show you around."

"Well now," Conway said, looking at Karen and Jonathan. "Don't I recognize you two? I do! You're the two who were on TV months ago with all that business about the hijacked shuttle and supposed creatures from space."

"Yes, yes," Blimpton said hurriedly, "that unfortunate hoax. But we have the shuttle back now and everything is fine."

"Oh, surely it couldn't all have been a hoax," the actor said, putting his hands on Karen's and Jonathan's shoulders. "I'm absolutely honored to meet you two. Whatever your story is, I'm sure it's fascinating. In fact, there's nothing I'd rather do than have a chat with you. What say we stop in at the ice-cream parlor up the street?"

"Well . . . uh, sure," Jonathan said. "I guess . . ."

"No, no. Sorry, Mr. Conway," Blimpton interrupted. "These two are very busy at the moment. Perhaps another time."

"Ah, but I won't be here another time. Such a busy filming schedule. What say we just dash out for a quick ice cream and a chat? I noticed they have a special on *peanut butter* milk shakes. I have a friend who's very fond of those."

Karen's expression fluttered between confusion and impossible hope. "Uh, yeah. Sounds great."

"Too bad there isn't time for it," Blimpton said firmly. "Now, Jonathan, Karen, we need to go out this way, please."

Conway kept his hands on the two children's shoulders. "Well, if you're going out, at least go up through the lobby. A couple of reporters and photographers came just to get some shots of Alex Greystone at the NASA office. I'm sure they'd love a shot of me with these two celebrities."

"That's absolutely out of the question!" Blimpton squeaked.

"No, what is absolutely out of the question is my leaving here without these two." Firmly, he started shepherding them down the corridor leading to the lobby.

Jonathan glanced back and whispered, "Hey, Mr. Conway, he's going for a phone."

The actor spun around and burst into the office. Blimpton's hand was on the telephone.

"Don't do that, Blimpton. I'm armed, you know."

The man's hand drew back, then he laughed. "Armed? You mean that toy ray gun of yours? I think this role-playing has gotten a bit much for you, Conway."

"No, not the movie prop," Conway said, pulling a small flat red triangle from his pocket. "I mean the real thing. And I've even had a crash course on how to use it."

Blimpton snorted. "A guitar pick? You've blown it, Conway." He lifted the receiver.

The actor thumbed a control, and a beam of pink light shot from the triangle and melted the phone.

"Come on, kids. Time's wasting."

The three turned and raced up the hall.

A minute later they walked into the lobby. "There he is!" a reporter yelled as a photographer snapped a picture. "Are those the important people you wanted us to meet?"

"Yes, you may remember them from that incident with the space shuttle last fall. It was, in fact, hijacked by a stranded UFO pilot."

More cameras clicked. Suddenly, several security guards strode up. "We're sorry, but we have orders to detain these individuals. The press must leave now."

"No way!" a reporter yelled. "Is someone trying to cover up something here?"

"Yes!" Jonathan shouted. "Just like before! They're trying to cover up a lot!"

Just then Vince, from Conway's studio, burst in. "Trevor, your limo driver said he'd left you here." He stopped and looked around at the reporters and the guards with their drawn guns. "What's going on?"

"A lot of deception is going on," the actor answered. "What I said this afternoon was wrong. That model is not from *Star Raiders Ten*. The rumors are probably right. If there are to be more *Star Raiders* movies, they probably aren't planned with Trevor Conway in them."

"Hey, Trevor," Vince said, "even if that's true, it's no reason for pulling some crazy publicity stunt."

"True. The real story is the cover-up of a true-life space drama. Last fall an alien crash-landed here, took the form of a skunk, was attacked by other aliens, and escaped in a space shuttle."

"Preposterous! Insane!" Mr. Blimpton shouted, while reporters scribbled frantically. "I'm afraid Mr. Conway has found the rumored end of his career too much for him and has lapsed into a fantasy world. And these two children are simply dupes. Now, if you will please . . ."

"Blimpton," the actor barked in his best Alex Greystone voice, "is this little space weapon a fantasy, too?" He held up the flat red triangle.

"Stop him!" Blimpton shrieked at the guards. "He's dangerous!"

"I can be," Conway said, aiming his weapon at the base of a tall metal sculpture at the side of the lobby. Its bottom section melted away. The metal tower toppled like a tree, smashing into a plate glass window. People ran, screaming.

Stunned, the actor stood staring at the weapon. Behind him, Karen tugged on his arm. "Mr. Conway, this is our chance. Time to do a real Hollywood escape."

"Right!" His head snapped up, and with a final sweep of the pink beam he took out all the lights in the lobby ceiling. The three raced for the broken window and leaped into the cool night air.

After a moment's shouting chaos, people began pouring out the door after them, photographers shooting pictures, and guards shooting high, warning shots. The three had just reached the sidewalk when a beam of bright pink light shot from the sky and melted a deep trench between them and their pursuers. Everyone looked up.

A sleek silver ship spiraled down and landed in the

street beside the man and two children. A door opened in the side, and a stout black-and-white skunk stared jauntily out.

"Stinker!" Karen and Jonathan ran over and would have hugged him if he hadn't warned them not to spoil the effect.

The only sound in the stunned silence was the clicking of cameras.

The actor raised his voice. "Still think this is a publicity stunt? Face it, it's the real thing. For generations we've dreamed of space adventure, but it's a dream no longer! We've already had a bit part in one space drama, and if we get our act together we can break into the big time!" Saluting the crowd, Conway joined the others and climbed into the ship.

"But wait!" a reporter called. "We've got questions. Lots of questions."

Karen looked back and shouted out, "Ask Mr. Blimpton. He likes questions. But don't let him cover anything up this time!" She turned to the skunk. "You have anything to add, Stinker?"

"Sure," Stinker broadcast into every mind there. "This is a pretty good planet you've got here. Sorry I can't stay and chat, but do let's keep in touch. It's been real."

With a final wave from the black-and-white tail, the door closed. In seconds, the silver ship swooped upward. Cameras clicked like crazed crickets.

Vince shook tears from his eyes. He turned to meet the stunned stare of the man from NASA. "I'd like to see them top *that* in Hollywood."

12

Over the Rainbow

"Might as well give them a real show," Stinker said from his seat at the instrument console. He pressed a control and the outside of the ship began glowing like a torch.

He sent the brilliant ship sailing low over Washington. It swooped around the Capitol dome, then glided along the Mall. A couple of loops around the Washington Monument, then it banked over the Lincoln Memorial and shot off toward the White House to fly slowly by the windows of the third floor. In a final flourish, it spiraled upward, looped into a somersault, then shot off like a backward meteor.

"So much for low profile." Karen laughed, wondering how they'd managed to do all that without feeling dizzy.

"Well," Stinker said, pointing his nose upward, "if you've got a high profile, might as well be up front about it."

"They sure can't cover up this visit," Jonathan said happily.

"Oh, but Stinker!" Karen said suddenly, "the Ruby Slippers! They took them back. What'll you do now? You're running out of time."

"No problem. I don't need them anymore. I've got something better."

"What?"

Stinker pointed a paw to where Trevor Conway sat studying the cabin in silent awe. "If the High Gyrn of Twak has seen *The Wizard of Oz*, he's surely seen *Star Raiders*. What could be more special for a movie buff than meeting Alex Greystone in person?"

"Wow, Mr. Conway," Jonathan said, "you're going off to that Twak planet?"

The actor gave them a slow, deep smile. "Hard to believe, isn't it? I'm actually going to visit the big cheese of a real interstellar empire."

With a worried frown, Karen turned to Stinker. "You're not going to let that wacky guy *keep* Mr. Conway, are you?"

"I doubt he'll want to. I didn't notice any real creatures in his collection. No, I figure we'll lay on the celebrity visit, maybe give him the 'authentic Star Raiders pistol' Conway's packing on his hip, then deliver Conway back to Hollywood."

The actor chuckled. "Once the press finishes with that, the studio will probably let me play Alex Greystone until I'm too old to move."

"And we'll go see every movie," Karen promised.

"So what about you two?" Stinker asked Karen and Jonathan. "I suppose we'd better get you back home so you can get on with your lives."

"Well . . ." Jonathan began, "things there ought to be better now that we're not world-class liars anymore. But, hey, our parents aren't expecting us for a few days yet."

"And I bet you could send them a message saying we'll be just a little longer," Karen added.

"Maybe," Stinker said, leaning back in his seat and clasping his paws behind his head. "So you'd like to come along and take a look at what things are like out there?" He waved a paw toward the star-filled view screen.

Their broad smiles were the only answer he needed.

"All right!" Eagerly, Stinker flopped himself forward and flashed little paws over the controls. "Let's boldly go where no humans and darn few skunks have gone before!"